UPDOG

WORLD'S GROSSEST

WORLD'S GROSSEST PLANTS

Scott Nickel

Lerner Publications ◆ Minneapolis

Lerner Publications Company
An imprint of Lerner Publishing Group, Inc.
241 First Avenue North
Minneapolis, MN 55401 USA

For reading levels and more information, look up this title at www.lernerbooks.com.

Main body text set in ITC Franklin Gothic Std.
Typeface provided by Adobe Systems.

Designer: Mary Ross
Lerner team: Sue Marquis

Library of Congress Cataloging-in-Publication Data

Names: Nickel, Scott, author.
Title: World's grossest plants / Scott Nickel.
Description: Minneapolis: Lerner Publications, [2022] | Series: World's grossest (updog books) | Includes bibliographical references and index. | Audience: Ages 8–11 | Audience: Grades K–1 | Summary: "Readers discover a jungle of repulsive plants in this gross guide! Learn about a flower that smells like rotting meat, a plant that swallows bugs, and much more." —Provided by publisher.
Identifiers: LCCN 2020009443 (print) | LCCN 2020009444 (ebook) | ISBN 9781728404011 (library binding) | ISBN 9781728418940 (ebook)
Subjects: LCSH: Plants—Miscellanea—Juvenile literature. | Flowers—Miscellanea—Juvenile literature.
Classification: LCC QK49 .N55 2021 (print) | LCC QK49 (ebook) | DDC 581—dc23

LC record available at https://lccn.loc.gov/2020009443
LC ebook record available at https://lccn.loc.gov/2020009444

Manufactured in the United States of America
1-48459-48973-6/11/2021

TABLE OF CONTENTS

POISONOUS PLANTS

Some plants are ugly or smelly. Some, like this hemlock, are deadly!

Berries from the doll's-eyes plant are poisonous.

POISONOUS:
dangerous to eat or touch

Oleander looks pretty,
but it makes you sick.

Deadly nightshade lives up to its name. Just two or three berries can kill you.

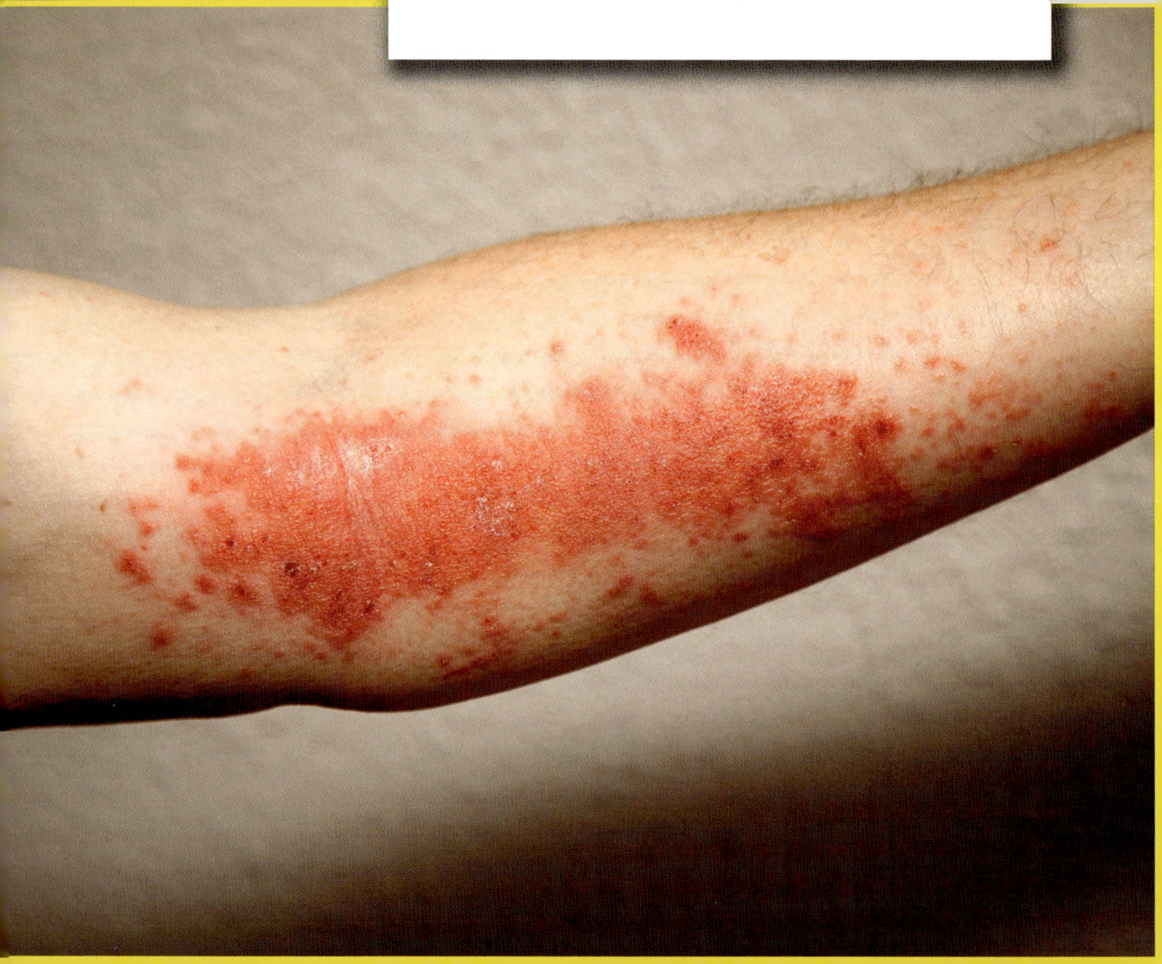

Poison ivy causes a red, itchy rash if it touches your skin.

The titan arum doesn't just smell like rotting meat. It's also poisonous.

UP NEXT!

FLOWERS THAT STINK.

FOUL FLOWERS

Valerian has pink flowers. But its roots smell like sweaty socks.

Does the stink lily stink? Yes! It smells like rotting flesh.

DISGUSTING DIAGRAM!

The stinking corpse lily is one of the smelliest flowers in the world.

CORPSE:
a dead body

lobe
central chamber
warts

WHICH IS **GROSSER?**

Octopus Stinkhorn vs. Skunk Cabbage

The octopus stinkhorn is a fungus. It smells so bad it attracts flies.

When skunk cabbage's leaves are bruised, it smells like skunk.

When ginkgo tree seeds decay, they can smell like poop.

DECAY:
rot and break down

UP NEXT!

KILLER PLANTS AND MORE.

GROSS GREENERY

Durian is a spiky fruit. Some think it smells like vomit.

Cedar-apple rust is a nasty plant sickness.

Plants can be carnivores. The restless flycatcher plant traps bugs.

CARNIVORE:
a living thing that eats animals to survive

It and other pitcher plants are filled with liquid that breaks down bugs.

Sundew plants use sticky tentacles to trap food.

Ugly, stinky, or deadly, plants like this titan arum are gross!

Glossary

carnivore: a living thing that eats animals to survive

corpse: a dead body

decay: rot and break down

poisonous: dangerous to eat or touch

Check It Out!

Botany Facts for Kids
https://kids.kiddle.co/Botany

Gross Science
https://www.pbs.org/show/gross-science/

Hirsch, Rebecca E. *When Plants Attack: Strange and Terrifying Plants.* Minneapolis: Millbrook Press, 2019.

Jose, Sarah. *Trees, Leaves, Flowers & Seeds: A Visual Encyclopedia of the Plant Kingdom.* New York: DK, 2019.

Markovics, Joyce. *Carnivorous Plants.* Ann Arbor, MI: Cherry Lake, 2022.

Meat-Eating Plants
https://kids.nationalgeographic.com/explore/science/meat-eating-plants

Index

Photo Acknowledgments

Image credits: Volodymyr Nikitenko/Shutterstock.com, p. 4; benet2006/flickr (CC BY 2.0), p. 5; Jim Evans/Wikimedia Commons (CC BY-SA 4.0), p. 6; Joan Simon/Wikimedia Commons (CC BY-SA 2.0), p. 7; James D Coppinger/Dembinsky Photo Associates/Alamy Stock Photo, p. 8; Richard J. Rehman/Wikimedia Commons (CC BY-SA 4.0), p. 9; H. Zell/Wikimedia Commons (CC BY-SA 3.0), pp. 10, 18; Jörg Hempel/Wikimedia Commons (CC BY-SA 3.0 DE), p. 11; SofianRafflesia/Wikimedia Commons (CC BY-SA 4.0), p. 13; Classiccardinal/Wikimedia Commons (CC BY-SA 3.0), p. 14 (top); Cephas/Wikimedia Commons (CC BY-SA 3.0), p. 14 (bottom); Famartin/Wikimedia Commons (CC BY-SA 4.0), pp. 15, 17; ىفنام/Wikimedia Commons (CC BY-SA 4.0), p. 16; MargaretRDonald/Wikimedia Commons (CC BY-SA 4.0), p. 19; Noah Elhardt/Wikimedia Commons (CC BY-SA 2.5), p. 20; Sailing moose/Wikimedia Commons (CC BY-SA 4.0), p. 21. Design elements: Saravudh Sudkhaw/Shutterstock.com; Green angel/Shutterstock.com.

Cover: Linas T/Shutterstock.com.